The Jungle Outside

T0309413

Written by Joanne C Hillhouse

Illustrated by Danielle Boodoo-Fortuné

Collins

"I wish I grew up in the jungle so I could know how to climb trees," Dante said.

Tanti turned from the dishes she'd been washing. Over the island that separated the kitchen from the living room, she spotted her grandson slumped on the living room couch looking like the unluckiest boy in the whole world. Larger than life on the TV, an animal clung to one tree limb while stretching towards another. A koala or sloth, she couldn't tell. They didn't have those in the Caribbean.

3

Tanti smiled.

"There's a jungle outside," she said.

"No, there isn't," Dante replied. "There's just the yard."

Tanti wiped her hands on a dish towel and walked to the door.

"Really?" She stepped outside.

Dante ran after her. She waited for him at the edge of the verandah with outstretched hand and eager grin.

"Ready?" she asked.

Dante knew it was just the yard but he still found himself nodding along, a smile splitting his face.

They stepped together bare foot into the yard. The grass was scratchy and uneven underfoot. He loved it.

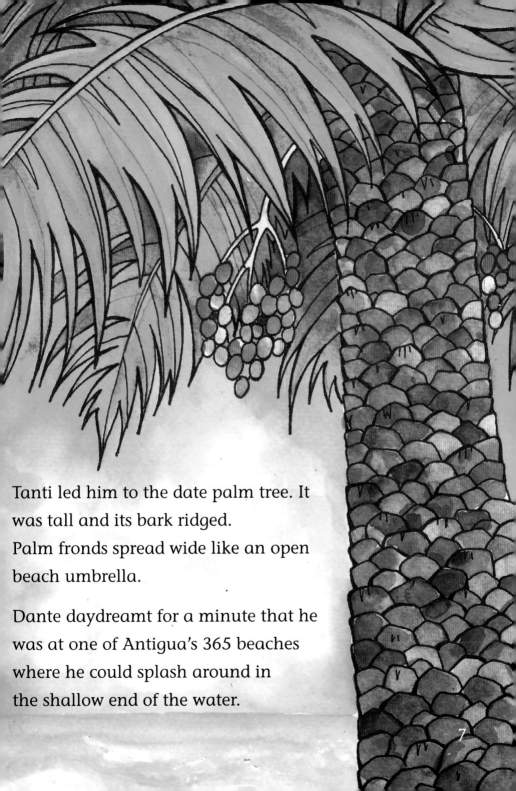

Tanti led him to the date palm tree. It was tall and its bark ridged.
Palm fronds spread wide like an open beach umbrella.

Dante daydreamt for a minute that he was at one of Antigua's 365 beaches where he could splash around in the shallow end of the water.

7

8

"When your daddy was little,"
Tanti said, "he climbed
this tree."

Dante looked up. The tree
was very, very tall.

"He'd seen men climbing
coconut trees by gripping
with their feet and knees and
pulling themselves up with
their upper body," Tanti said.
"My heart nearly jumped out
of my chest when I saw him
up there. His too, I think, when
he realised that what goes
up must come back down."
She laughed. "As you can see,
the date palm bark isn't smooth
like a coconut tree. Not so easy
to slide back down. One day,
you must ask your daddy if
the two dates he picked were
worth all the scratches."

9

Dante tilted his head to try to see all
the way up the date palm tree. Sun
leaked between the bladed leaves.
He tried to picture his daddy as
a boy. He couldn't. He also couldn't
picture himself up this or any
other tree. Imagine being that high
up and having to get back down.

Dante backed away from
the big tree.

Tanti chuckled. "Come," she said.

There were two date palm trees in Tanti's yard, plus
a guava tree, a tall pawpaw tree, a sweet-sweet soursop
tree, three mango trees, a Caribbean cherry tree,
a lemon tree, a turkleberry tree, which Tanti said
was used for sticking kites, banana trees and,
in the ground, sweet potato, pumpkin
and watermelon. Dante had never paid attention to
them before.

Tanti walked him towards the oldest, sweetest and biggest of the mango trees. It wasn't as tall as the date palm tree, but it was wide, limbs stretching crookedly in every direction, covered in leaves. Mangoes were starting to come in, but they were high up still.

Dante felt his mouth water. He loved mangoes and this tree he had dreamt of climbing. He was scared though. It was so broad, so big.

The lower branches sprouted pale yellow mango blossoms. If high winds didn't knock them off, they'd turn into fruits that even he could reach.

The high fruit was for the birds. "What the birds don't peck up high, the dogs run off with down low," Dante had heard his grandma gripe more than once. Everybody knew mongooses ate everything but who knew even dogs liked mangoes.

"Want to climb?" Tanti asked. "When I was little like you, mangoes couldn't fall before I get to them."

She pointed. "You see those limbs high up." He did. He saw the way the strong breeze didn't just flutter the leaves but caused the limbs themselves to wave. "All up there I reach," Tanti said.

"You weren't afraid to fall?" Dante asked.

"Can't think about falling or you'll never climb," Tanti replied.

"Know what you have to think of?"

Dante looked up at her, eyes wide, and shook his head.

She smiled, drawing out each adjective as she spoke: "... the big, fat, ripe, juicy, sweet mango."

Dante was dribbling like he hadn't since he was a baby.

"We climbed every tree as children," Tanti said, looking around the yard. She grew everything in it herself, tending it while dressed in her old boots and older straw hat. "Walking home from school, nothing missed us – not raspberry, not plum, not dumms, not tamarind, not even stinking toe. And during the summer, there was so much mango, and bright orange plum, and gynep with the slick pink covering and the crunchy seed at the centre, we could never go hungry. It wasn't good to eat too much though." She rubbed her stomach and pulled a pained face.

"Too much of anything is never good."

Dante tried to picture his grandma as a girl running and climbing trees. He could kind of see it; Tanti was the kind of grandma who played hand tennis with him in the street outside the house and jumped rope with him on the back verandah.

Her fun side peeked out as she said, "What you say, you want to climb?" in a voice that made her sound like one of his friends from school instead of his grandma.

Dante looked up. He wanted
to climb so, so bad, but it
was so high.

"Come, I'll help you," Tanti said. She cupped her hands and bent over to give him a boost.

Dante hesitated. Tanti waited with her hands cupped, as though they had all the time in the world. Time ticked on. Dante tried to find his nerve. Tanti shook her cupped hands. He saw that they were clasped tight-tight and knew she would not let him fall.

"OK," he said, locking eyes with her, as he raised his leg to step up into her arms.

Dante's grandma hoisted
him easily on to one of
the low branches.

"Don't worry, I'm right here,"
she said. "And look, there's
a mango right there."

He looked to where
she pointed.

20

It was a stretch.

He took a breath.

He didn't look down. He looked at the big, fat, ripe, juicy, sweet mango as he stretched for it.

He overreached.

21

Tanti was there to catch him, and she laughed with him when he held up his prize.

"Got it!" said Dante.

Tanti grinned. "You are about to discover something only true island people know," she said.

"What?" Dante asked, as Tanti set him down.

"Nothing sweeter than fruit you pick with your own hand."

She took the mango, bounced it, as though weighing it. "Big one," she said. "Go ahead, bite."

And he did. Tanti was right. It was the best mango he had ever tasted. He ate it off clean.

Something else only true island people know, even little boys like Dante: the right way to eat a mango. Bite into it and suck the fruit all the way down to the seed. Your hands and your face might get sticky but that was all part of the fun. Dante was sticky down to his elbows by the time the mango seed was white, no more juice to be found.

While he ate, Tanti had been busy stretching and plucking a few mangoes of her own.

Dante wondered why he
had waited so long to climb
a mango tree.

The sweet memory of his climb
up the mango tree fresh in his
mind, he looked around
the yard. He saw, as if with
new eyes, how thick it was:
like a jungle. He saw, too,
how much ripened fruit
there was to be plucked.

Dante pointed to the top of the tall papaya tree, what people on the island called pawpaw or pupa. "Look, Tanti, a ripe one. Lift me up, lift me up."

Laughing, Dante's grandma did just that.

Dante felt happy and could not think what could make this day better. He sat up suddenly.

"Tanti, can you show me how to make a kite with the turkleberry?"

"Oh, now you're interested," she teased.

Not long ago, Tanti had mentioned making a kite. Dante had been too busy with his latest video game to pay attention. Now, he couldn't imagine anything more exciting. Tanti had said all it took was spine from a couple of the leaves from the dwarf coconut tree near the back fence.

"Tie two into a 't' with thread, shape old newspaper over that and glue into a diamond shape with turkleberry; old scraps of cloth for a tail."

He could take it to the kite festival to fly.

Tanti would help. "Of course," she said, hugging Dante, with a chuckle. "Of course, I will. But that's an adventure for another day."

Dante's jungle journey

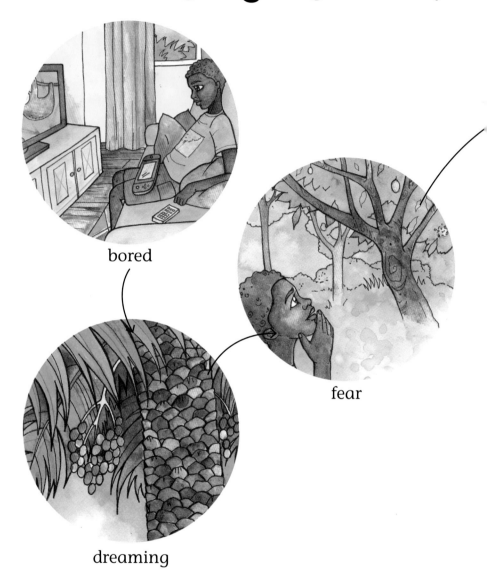

bored

fear

dreaming

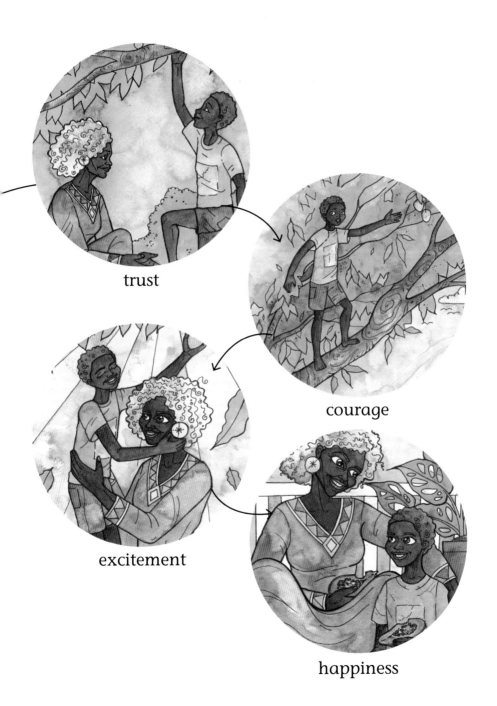

trust

courage

excitement

happiness

Ideas for reading

Written by Christine Whitney
Primary Literacy Consultant

Reading objectives:
- discuss the sequence of events in books

- make inferences on the basis of what is being said and done

- predict what might happen on the basis of what has been read so far

Spoken language objectives:
- ask relevant questions

- speculate, imagine and explore ideas through talk

- participate in discussions

Curriculum links: Science – use the local environment to explore plants growing in their habitat; Writing – write narratives about personal experiences and those of others, write for different purposes

Interest words: palm fronds, bladed leaves, verandah

Word count: 1489

Resources: paper and pencils, a selection of fruits for tasting

Build a context for reading

- Ask children what they know about the following trees: date palm, pawpaw, turkleberry, guava, soursop.

- Turn to pp2–3 and look at the image of Dante slumped on a couch, looking sad and watching TV. Before they read p3, ask children to talk about what they think Dante is wishing for. Children could write their ideas in a thought bubble.

- Read the blurb on the back cover. Ask children to discuss their own fears. Have their fears ever held them back from doing something they would like to do?